Nana
the Outfield

By Janet Mitchell
Illustrated by Lisa Adams

Outskirts Press, Inc.
http://www.outskirtspress.com

ISBN: 978-1-4787-9492-9

Illustrated by Lisa Adams

Outskirts Press and the "OP" logo are trademarks belonging to Outskirts Press, Inc.

PRINTED IN THE UNITED STATES OF AMERICA

For Ruth Koenigsberg, an
extraordinary educator who
encouraged all of her students to
play with joy for the love of the game.

SOPHIE WAS EXCITED! TODAY AT SCHOOL, EVERYONE IN HER CLASS WAS GOING TO TELL ABOUT THEIR GRANDMOTHER.

SOPHIE LOVED HER GRANDMOTHER SO MUCH. BUT NANA LIVED FAR AWAY. SOPHIE MOSTLY ONLY GOT TO SEE NANA ON FACETIME.

SHE THOUGHT OF HER FAVORITE
THINGS TO SAY ABOUT NANA
AND COULD HARDLY WAIT FOR
SHARING TIME TO START.
FINALLY, AFTER WORKING
HARD ALL MORNING, HER
TEACHER, MISS KLODT, SAID,
"GRANDMOTHER SHARING TIME
HAS ARRIVED!"

STEVEN SHOWED THE BRIGHTLY COLORED SWEATER THAT HIS GRAMMY MADE ESPECIALLY FOR HIM.

MADISON TOLD ABOUT HOW HER GRANDMOTHER OWNS A COMPANY AND HAS LOTS OF PEOPLE WORKING FOR HER.

ANGIE BROUGHT IN A BIG PLATE OF SUGAR COOKIES – WITH SPRINKLES – THAT HER MEEMAW MADE FOR THE WHOLE CLASS.

JACK SAID THAT HIS GRANNY LOVED TO PLAY THE PIANO AND SING WITH HIM.

FINALLY, IT WAS SOPHIE'S TURN. SHE TOLD THE CLASS, "I CALL MY GRANDMOTHER 'NANA', AND SHE LOVES TO PLAY SOFTBALL, JUST LIKE ME!"

EVERYONE LAUGHED!! SOPHIE WAS SO SURPRISED. SHE WASN'T SURE WHAT TO DO.

MISS KLODT TOLD EVERYONE TO QUIET DOWN AND ASKED SOPHIE TO TELL THE CLASS ABOUT NANA PLAYING SOFTBALL.

"SOFTBALL IS LIKE BASEBALL, EXCEPT WITH A BIGGER BALL. THE PITCHER THROWS THE BALL UNDERHAND INSTEAD OF OVERHAND. MY NANA'S TEAM HAS LOTS OF GRANDMOTHERS AND THEY ALL LOVE TO PLAY. MY OWN TEAM IS ALL LITTLE KIDS."

"I DON'T THINK GRANDMOTHERS REALLY PLAY SOFTBALL," AARON SAID. "YES, THEY DO!" CRIED SOPHIE. SHE RETURNED TO HER DESK AND WAS VERY DISAPPOINTED.

THAT NIGHT, SOPHIE TOLD HER MOM THAT SHE WAS SAD ABOUT WHAT HAPPENED AT SCHOOL. "THE KIDS DIDN'T BELIEVE ME," SHE SAID. "I WISH I COULD TALK TO NANA."

SOPHIE'S MOM ASKED, "HOW WOULD YOU LIKE TO GO WATCH NANA PLAY SOFTBALL WITH HER TEAM?"

"OH, YES!!" SOPHIE SQUEALED. SHE AND HER MOM WOULD FLY ON AN AIRPLANE TO ANOTHER CITY AND WATCH NANA'S TEAM PLAY IN A SENIOR SOFTBALL TOURNAMENT. THEY WOULD SEE A WHOLE BUNCH OF GRANDMOTHERS PLAYING SOFTBALL — WOW!!

SOPHIE WAS SO EXCITED.
THE NEXT DAY SHE TOLD HER
CLASSMATES ABOUT HER TRIP.
THEY THOUGHT IT SOUNDED
LIKE FUN, BUT STILL DID NOT
BELIEVE THAT GRANDMOTHERS
PLAYED SOFTBALL. SOPHIE
PROMISED TO BRING BACK SOME
PICTURES TO PROVE IT.

AFTER TWO WEEKS IT WAS TIME
TO GO! SOPHIE AND HER MOM
GOT ON THE AIRPLANE AND FLEW
TO A BIG CITY IN CALIFORNIA
TO WATCH NANA PLAY SOFTBALL.

SOPHIE AND HER MOM STAYED
IN A HOTEL THAT HAD BIG
FLUFFY PILLOWS ON THE BED
AND A SWIMMING POOL WITH A
SLIDING BOARD. AFTER A GOOD
NIGHT'S SLEEP, SOPHIE PUT
ON HER RED AND BLACK SHIRT
SO SHE WOULD MATCH NANA'S
TEAM UNIFORM, AND THEY
HEADED OFF TO THE SOFTBALL
FIELDS.

THERE WERE 8 FIELDS AT THE PARK, AND SOFTBALL GAMES GOING ON EVERYWHERE! "NANA'S TEAM IS PLAYING ON FIELD #2," SAID MOM. "WE'LL GO STRAIGHT THERE."

THE GAME ON FIELD #2 HAD ALREADY STARTED. SOPHIE LOOKED ALL OVER FOR NANA BUT COULD NOT FIND HER. "MOM, I DON'T SEE NANA - WHERE IS SHE?" SOPHIE ASKED.

"NANA'S IN THE OUTFIELD," MOM TOLD HER. "RIGHT OUT THERE IN CENTER FIELD."

JUST THEN THE BATTER HIT THE BALL WAY OUT TO CENTER FIELD. NANA TOOK OFF RUNNING, LOOKED OVER HER SHOULDER, AND REACHED UP TO CATCH THE BALL. EVERYONE CHEERED, ESPECIALLY SOPHIE.

"THAT'S MY NANA!!" SHE YELLED. "GOOOOOOOOO NANA!"

AFTER 3 OUTS, NANA'S TEAM JOGGED OFF THE FIELD AND INTO THE DUGOUT. SOPHIE RAN OVER AND HUGGED NANA AS HARD AS SHE COULD. "GREAT CATCH, NANA! YOU'RE A STAR!"

NANA LAUGHED. "IT'S NOT IMPORTANT TO BE A STAR. IT'S IMPORTANT TO TRY YOUR BEST, SUPPORT YOUR TEAMMATES, STAY POSITIVE AND HAVE FUN, NO MATTER WHAT HAPPENS." AND THEN NANA CALLED TO HER TEAMMATES, "HEY EVERYONE - THIS IS MY WONDERFUL GRANDDAUGHTER, SOPHIE."

SOPHIE RETURNED TO HER SEAT TO WATCH THE REST OF THE GAME. NANA'S TEAM HAD A LOT OF GRANDMOTHERS. THEY ALL RAN HARD, TRIED THEIR BEST TO CATCH, THROW AND HIT THE BALL, AND CHEERED FOR THEIR TEAMMATES. NANA'S TEAM WON THE GAME 8-5. IT WAS VERY EXCITING!

"NANA, MY CLASSMATES DON'T BELIEVE THAT GRANDMOTHERS PLAY SOFTBALL," SOPHIE TOLD HER GRANDMOTHER.

"ON MY TEAM, EVERYONE IS AT LEAST 60 YEARS OLD, AND MANY OF US ARE GRANDMOTHERS," NANA TOLD HER. "WE ALL LOVE TO STAY ACTIVE AND SPEND TIME PLAYING BALL GAMES WITH OUR FRIENDS. IT'S SO MUCH FUN, AND IT KEEPS US HEALTHY. I'VE BEEN PLAYING SOFTBALL SINCE I WAS A LITTLE GIRL, JUST LIKE YOU."

SOPHIE CHEERED FOR NANA'S TEAM ALL WEEKEND, AND NOBODY WAS MORE EXCITED TO SEE THEM FINISH IN FIRST PLACE AND WIN A GOLD MEDAL. SOPHIE TOOK A LOT OF PICTURES TO SHOW HER CLASSMATES.

"NANA, I CAN'T WAIT TO SHOW MY FRIENDS THESE PHOTOS OF YOUR TEAM. THEN THEY WILL BELIEVE ME WHEN I SAY MY NANA PLAYS SOFTBALL."

"LET'S DO EVEN MORE THAN THAT," SAID NANA. SHE TOOK OFF HER GOLD MEDAL AND HANDED IT TO SOPHIE.

"I WANT YOU TO KEEP THIS AS A REMINDER TO ALWAYS STAY ACTIVE, PLAY HARD, TRY YOUR BEST, AND HAVE FUN. YOU MIGHT EVEN BE PLAYING WHEN YOU BECOME A GRANDMOTHER!"

SOPHIE HELD NANA'S HAND AND SAID, "DON'T WORRY, NANA. I WILL ALWAYS PLAY SOFTBALL AND TRY MY BEST, JUST LIKE YOU."

SOPHIE WORE HER GOLD MEDAL BACK TO THE HOTEL, ALL NIGHT WHILE SHE SLEPT, AND THEN ON THE AIRPLANE AS THEY FLEW BACK HOME.

THE NEXT DAY IN SCHOOL,
SOPHIE'S CLASSMATES CROWDED
AROUND TO SEE THE GOLD
MEDAL AND LOOK AT THE
PICTURES.

THEY ALL AGREED THAT SOPHIE
HAS THE COOLEST GRANDMOTHER
EVER!

Author's Note:

Are you interested in playing senior softball? There are senior softball tournaments and organizations all over the United States and Canada. It's a great way to stay active and have fun at the same time!

For information, search the internet for 'senior softball'. Find a team and join the fun!

CPSIA information can be obtained at www.ICGtesting.com
Printed in the USA
BVIW12n2326240518
517064BV00001B/2